Barker's Doghouse: Leave It!

Maria Bea Alfano

Illustrated by Laura Catalán

PIXEL+INK

PIXEL✛INK

Pixel+Ink is an imprint of TGM Development Corp.

Text and all illustrations copyright © 2025 by TGM Development Corp.
Text written by Maria Bea Alfano
Jacket and interior illustrations by Laura Catalán
All rights reserved. No part of this book may be reproduced, transmitted, or stored in an information retrieval system in any form or by any means, graphic, electronic, or mechanical, including photocopying, taping, and recording, without prior written permission from the publisher. Additionally, no part of this book may be used or reproduced in any manner for the purpose of training artificial intelligence technologies or systems, nor for text and data mining.
Printed and bound in September 2025 at Sheridan, Chelsea, MI, U.S.A.
Book design by Nicole Gureli
www.pixelandinkbooks.com
First Edition
ISBN: 978-1-64595-272-5 | 1 3 5 7 9 10 8 6 4 2 (hardcover)
ISBN: 978-1-64595-288-6 | 1 3 5 7 9 10 8 6 4 2 (paperback)

Library of Congress Cataloging-in-Publication Data is available.

EU Authorized Representative: HackettFlynn Ltd, 36 Cloch Choirneal, Balrothery, Co. Dublin, K32 C942, Ireland. EU@walkerpublishinggroup.com

FOR MY MOM, WHO'D BURST AT THE SEAMS ANY TIME SHE HAD A SURPRISE FOR ME

CHAPTER ONE

Mornings

"GioGioGio! Ruffruffruff, arooo!"

Gio heard his friend Millie calling for him even before he walked up the front steps.

Poom! Poom! Her front paws pounded against the inside of the door. He imagined her furry black-and-white body leaping up as high as the doorknob.

Nah, she can jump higher, Gio thought with a smile.

The tiny mini-schnauzer and toy poodle mix was only as tall as his shin, but she gave big-dog vibes.

"GioGioGio!" Millie called from behind the door. "Wait till you hear!"

Gio had started picking her up in the mornings and bringing her back to Barker's Doghouse, the doggy daycare his mom ran out of their house.

It was the best way to get the day's scoop before he left for school.

Last summer, Gio and his mom had moved to Milton from the town where he'd grown up—the place where all his friends still were. His mom was supposed to take care of his Grandpa Lou, but then Grandpa Lou died.

And instead of moving back home, Gio's mom had opened a daycare for dogs in his grandpa's living room!

Its slogan was "Barker's Doghouse—When you stay with us, you stay with family!"

Or, as Gio always joked, "Stay in my house. Eat all my snacks. Chew up my sneakers."

Gio didn't like that his mom had moved them to Milton. And he didn't like that Barker's Doghouse was all she seemed to care about. But he did love the dogs. Sometimes it seemed like they were his only friends in this new place . . . plus they were an excellent network of spies.

"Happy Friday! Have I got some news for you!" Millie squealed as the door creaked open. She burst out at him, dragging her leash and a pack full of supplies for the day. Then she whimpered and rolled over onto her back for scritches.

Gio's classmate Isa—who also happened to be Millie's person—peeked around the door behind her. She was still wearing her pajamas and her straight black hair stuck out all over the place.

Isa was always pulled-together and bubbly at school, but she was *not* a morning person.

"Um, hi," Gio said. Even though he ate lunch with Isa and her friend Evie most days, he didn't feel like they were *friends* friends yet. And it was weird to see her in zombie mode.

"Uun," Isa grunted as she handed over Millie's favorite squeaky banana.

Millie jumped for it and shouted, "Mine!"

Gio let Millie tug on the toy for a minute before tucking it safely into her doggy backpack.

Then Millie sprung up and boomeranged her front paws off Gio's thigh. "I saw your teacher's dog at the park last night. His breath is rank. Anyway . . . he told me you have a spelling test first thing today. Don't forget to tell Isa!"

Everything Millie was saying sounded like barks and whimpers to most people, but not to Gio. Gio

understood dogs when they spoke to him—as if they were using human words.

It had all started when Gio accidentally ate a dog treat his mom had made. The treat looked and smelled like a peanut butter cookie but was secretly stuffed with—ew!—lamb lung.

He still didn't know what kind of magic made it happen, but he had this superpower now. And he wanted to keep it a secret.

"So I heard we're going to have a spelling test," Gio repeated to Isa.

Isa pushed her messy bangs off her forehead.

"How do you even know these things?" she asked.

She shook her head at Gio. Then she bent down to say good-bye to Millie. The schnoodle whined and pressed the side of her body into Isa's leg.

"Don't worry, Milsie, I'll see you tonight and we'll have adventures." She looked deep into Millie's eyes and rubbed behind her ears. Millie licked Isa's nose.

Gio looked away uncomfortably.

After a few seconds, Millie piped up with, "Tell Isa not to forget her oboe. She has lessons right after school today!" Millie loved having jobs to do, and keeping track of Isa was one of them.

Gio rubbed the back of his neck. Being their go-between felt awkward sometimes.

Isa could *not* speak to dogs. So far, Gio was the only person he knew who could.

"Hey, Isa, is today the day you have oboe after school?" Gio asked.

"My oboe! I totally forgot!" Isa popped up and ran inside to put the instrument next to her backpack. Gio heard books falling and Isa's grandma shouting for her to eat breakfast.

He clipped Millie's pup-pack onto her back and they headed down the stairs.

"This will be so much easier once Isa eats one of those dog treats your mom made that one time," Millie said. "Then I can tell her all this stuff myself. And the three of us can hang out and share our deepest secrets." She did a little jump-spin. "Why doesn't your mom make those treats all the time?"

That sounded awkward, too. Gio wasn't sure he was up for sharing his friends—or his secret—like

that. He didn't even know if his mom's treats would work for Isa. But Millie had high hopes.

"Let's go to the park after school," Millie suggested as they started walking toward Barker's Doghouse. "I heard Gabe has detention all week, so he won't be there."

Gabe was a bully and Gio tried to stay away from him. Millie always knew exactly which secrets to share. She was a good friend.

"That sounds like fun," he told her. As they rounded the corner toward Barker's Doghouse, Gio glanced around to make sure no one could see him talking to a dog. Then he got straight to his point.

"But let's talk about my birthday... have you sniffed anything out yet?"

"Um, well, sort of... But first I have to tell you something before I forget. It's impor—"

But Gio was distracted by shouting.

"Red alert! Red alert! Emergency!" A little brown chiweenie—a Chihuahua and dachshund mix with tiny legs and a long body—was howling from inside the window of Barker's.

"What's going on, Houdini?" Gio asked as they ran toward the front steps.

Millie answered for the other dog. "Oh, that's what I was going to tell you," she said. "Your mom is on her way home with a puppy!"

CHAPTER TWO

Gio felt deflated, like a balloon that someone couldn't tie fast enough. "A puppy?"

Don't we have enough dogs? he thought. He loved his pack, but another dog felt more like a present for his mom. And it was going to be *his* birthday.

Every year his mom found a way to surprise him, and this year, Gio knew exactly what he wanted his surprise to be. He wanted to go back to his old town to spend his birthday with his home friends!

So Gio was trying to figure out what she was planning. And his doggy spies had agreed to help him. Except they hadn't found anything out yet. His mom was that good.

"I don't think it's for your birthday," Millie said. "So don't worry." But that didn't make Gio feel much better. Why did his mom keep doing things without telling him?

"ETA ten minutes and counting!" Houdini called.

Millie yanked at her leash. "We gotta get inside, Gio," she said. "This is serious."

Gio unclipped her pup-pack, opened the door, and kicked off his sneakers.

Millie burst into the house like she was on a cooking show and only had 3.5 seconds to grab all the ingredients.

"Begin Puppy Protocol 6.1!" she directed as she leaped over the baby gate that separated the front hallway from the living room.

"Tell your mom not to let it in here," Felix griped. "Tell her we're allergic!"

Felix, a shaggy old dog with an underbite, hated any kind of change.

"Tell your mom it will get abducted by aliens if it stays here!" Houdini slid down off the couch and nipped at Gio's ankles. Houdini was an escape artist who loved conspiracy theories.

Most of the dogs had just been dropped off, but

the living room already looked like a kindergarten classroom right before recess.

Gio remembered when his grandpa used to tell him stories in the big green armchair. Now it was a big green doggy bed. Moose, a Great Dane the size of a horse, was already dozing off on it.

Gary, the mini-greyhound, was perched on one of the arms, looking out the window. His job was to bark as soon as Gio's mom's car pulled into the driveway.

"Hide all your favorite toys!" Millie bellowed. "Bury your chews!" Millie was good at taking charge. It was another one of her jobs.

Houdini pawed at a floorboard until it came loose. She pushed a bunch of toys inside and then pulled the board back in place with her teeth.

"No, that's *my* secret spot!" Millie whined. She nipped at Houdini's tail and Houdini snapped back, snagging an ear between her teeth.

"Yeow!" Millie howled.

Gio shrank away. Sure, he could talk to dogs, but he didn't always understand the things they did.

While the two dogs wrestled, Felix piled his water

bowl and chew toys onto a cushion. Then he bit down on it and dragged everything into the corner between the couch and the wall. He used a few pillows to wall himself in like a fort.

"Wake me when it's grown!" he said.

Will my things be safe upstairs? Gio wondered. The dogs were supposed to stay on the first floor, but once in a while they snuck up into the bedrooms.

Gio turned to see the daycare's sheepdog, Avocado, bound in from the backyard dragging their soccer goal. Gio and the dogs *loved* playing soccer together.

"Do me a favor, Sport, and hide this," Avocado called. "And put some muscle in that hustle!"

Gio tried shoving the goal under the dining room table, but Avocado used his body to block him.

"Not there, Sport! Higher up where the little land shark can't reach." Avocado nudged his head against Gio's leg. "You sure you wanna leave your sneakers there?"

"What do you mean, *there*?" Gio asked. "My sneakers are on my feet."

"Your toes, your loss," Avocado answered, and then ran back out to the yard.

"Puppies piddle on sneakers," Felix called from his corner.

"They piddle on *everything*!" Millie added.

"What is happening right now?" asked Gio. "Are we getting a puppy or a wrecking ball?"

Gio caught himself and lowered his voice. His mom's teenaged assistant, Janice, was in the kitchen looking for snacks.

She couldn't know he talked to the dogs. She'd

post his secret all over social media, and he didn't want to be internet famous. How would he ever make new friends then?

"Don't worry, Gio," Millie said. "It's not as bad as it looks. Puppies can be very sweet but we still have to be careful—or we'll lose our favorite toys!"

"Or an ear!" shouted Felix from behind his fort.

"Are you sure Mom said the word *puppy* and not like . . . ?" Gio asked. But he couldn't think of a word that sounded like puppy but was actually something good. "Look, I have to get to school. I have that surprise spelling test. I'll be back to help out this afternoon, okay?"

The truth was he didn't feel ready to meet some puppy—or to see his mom. Everything was so different here in Milton. His best friends were dogs. He might not get to go home for his birthday. And there was a bully who made Gio feel like danger lurked around every turn.

He was tired of so many changes!

"Wait, Gio." Millie pulled the squeaky banana out of her pup-pack with her teeth. "Take this to school

with you. Give it to Isa. You've gotta protect it, Gio Barker. You're my only hope!"

Gio zipped her toy banana safely into his backpack. It was all he could do for his friend right now.

"Don't worry," Gio said. "You can count on me."

But what could Gio count on coming home to?

CHAPTER THREE

Meet the Land Shark

After school, Gio pushed open the gate to the backyard, ready for the dogs to jump on him like they always did. Their greetings made him feel like *every* day was his birthday.

But the yard was weirdly quiet today, and kind of messy. The grass was torn up in patches, broken toys were scattered everywhere, and one of the wooden posts had been almost chewed off the back porch.

Most of the daycare dogs were lying on their sides in the grass with their tongues hanging out. Millie, Gary, Houdini, and even the big old Great Dane, Moose... but none of them barked or jumped or moved at all.

Gio was worried. *What happened to them?* he wondered.

"Send it back," Houdini mumbled in her sleep.

As Gio tiptoed closer, Moose lifted his head, then let it drop as if it were too heavy to hold up. Millie's back leg twitched like she was running in her sleep. One eye opened as he got closer.

"Gio, is that you?" she asked.

"Millie, are you okay?" he asked back. But she didn't answer.

Gary, the mini-greyhound, crawled toward Gio on three paws.

"Get out while you still can," he warned.

Gio scanned the yard for the danger.

He spotted Avocado lying next to a cage. And curled up inside the cage was a puppy, fast asleep.

The puppy was barely bigger than one of Gio's stuffies, with dark brown fur that looked just as soft. He seemed so peaceful, it was hard to imagine him creating a path of destruction. Okay, Gio had to admit it: the pup was adorable.

Avocado hobbled over for some pets before settling back down in the grass next to the cage.

"I'm on guard duty," the big sheepdog told Gio.

"Best gig ever, Sport. All I have to do is sit here and look at the newbie without barking or pouncing and I get a treat."

That was great for Avocado, but what about everyone else?

Just then, Gio's mom came out of the house with fresh water and treats for everyone.

"You're home!" she said to Gio, as if she were surprised.

"What happened to the dogs?" Gio asked.

"They may have gotten a little too much Bean today," she said.

Gio dropped his backpack in the grass. "You fed them beans?"

"No, *Bean*." She cocked her head toward the puppy in the cage. "He's a chocolate Labrador retriever. His name is Bean. Short for Bean Burrito. He had the dogs running all day long."

"Got it," Gio said. He crept closer to the cage. "So . . . why's he in jail?

Gio's mom smiled. "The crate is his safe space—kind of like your bedroom is for you. Crate-training helps him learn how to settle down after exercise, how to be alone, and how to go potty in the right spot. If he's in there, he's not peeing on things out here."

Ever since she opened the daycare, his mom had talked nonstop about peeing.

"You're so cringe, Mom," Gio said.

His mom shrugged. He was always saying that.

"When we let him out, Bean should go straight to the corner to potty," she said. "He's learning fast. Wanna see?"

Bean lifted his head at the sound of his name and yawned. Maybe he did have the teeth of a land shark, but they were tiny and perfect.

Gio watched as his mom eased open the door of the crate. The puppy slowly stood up and stretched out his front legs, raising his hind end in the air.

Then he blinked a few times and waddled over to the corner of the yard, where he lifted his leg and peed on the fence post.

As soon as he was done, he bounded back toward Gio. His tongue was hanging out and his tail wagged. He wasn't big now, but he was going to get way bigger judging by the size of his paws.

"Whoa, he's cute," Gio said almost without thinking.

Millie perked up her head. "Be careful, Gio," she said. "He bites."

Gio just ignored her. When he sat down next to the crate, Bean pounced on him and licked his face.

"Aw, hello Beanie," Gio said. He scratched Bean's bum and looked back up at his mom. "His hair is so soft. Ouch!" Gio pulled his hand back from Bean's sharp teeth. "My hand is not a chew toy!"

Houdini laughed an evil villain kind of laugh.

"We warned you!" said Gary.

"Who's cute now?" Millie muttered.

Bean started sniffing around Gio's backpack. Gio could see his tiny nostrils moving in and out, following a scent.

Then Bean stuck his little brown snout inside the front flap and Gio saw a flash of yellow. Millie's squeaky banana! Gio quickly pulled the backpack closer to him so Bean couldn't get it.

Millie crawled over to Gio and pawed at his hand. "Gio, let's go to the park," she said.

You can hardly move, Gio thought. *And I'm meeting Bean.* But Millie couldn't read his mind and Gio had to be careful what he said around his mom. The last time he'd spoken to the dogs in front of his mother, she'd gotten all worried and threatened to talk to his teacher!

Millie whined and pawed at him again. While he was distracted, Bean nipped his toes.

"Ouch! Not now, Millie," Gio snapped. He grabbed a treat from his mom and tossed it across the lawn for her to go find.

Millie glared at Gio like she was blasting him with

laser vision. Then she dashed off to find the treat.

Gio's mom wiggled a stuffed dinosaur and Bean ran over to chomp on it.

"He's teething and it hurts," she said. "Chewing makes him feel better. You were the same way as a baby. If you don't want your hand to be a chew toy, just give him something else to chew on."

Avocado raised his head. "I like to chew on sticks."

"I quite enjoy gnawing the bones of my captors," Houdini added.

"I'm so glad you don't sleep here," Gio said to Houdini. Then he caught himself and glanced up at his mom. *Had she noticed?*

"What was that?" his mom asked.

Gio gave her his best blank stare

"Actually, the puppy *will* be sleeping here," his mom said. "We're fostering him for the local shelter."

Gio must have looked really confused, because she continued to explain.

"We're basically training him and taking care of him until the shelter finds a family to adopt him." She handed Bean a raw carrot to chew on. The puppy

grabbed it between his teeth, tail wagging, and took it back inside his crate.

"Wait a minute. You brought me a puppy for my birthday and then you're just going to give it away?" Gio asked.

"Oh no, honey, Bean's not your birthday surprise. I would never do that to you!" Gio's mom winked at him. "You'll never guess what your birthday surprise is!"

Phew! Gio thought. There was still a chance he'd get to see his friends!

"Never say never," he said. It had always been one of his grandpa's favorite sayings.

Gio's mom began to sing a Taylor Swift tune. "You'll never ever ever *everrrr*…guess your present." She sat back and laughed.

He threw the stuffed dinosaur at her.

"Cringe," he said.

CHAPTER FOUR

Birthday Plans

"Do you really think your mom is going to let you come here for your birthday?" Gio's friend Charlotte—aka Char or CharChar—leaned close to the camera so all Gio could see on his computer screen was the blur of her brown eye.

"Yeah," said Jonah. "We *have* to spend your birthday together. It's tradition!"

Gio was on a video call with his best friends from forever, Marco, Char, and Jonah. He sat on his bed while they all hung out in Char's basement.

He missed getting to hang out with his friends in person, but he liked that they still made time to see him virtually. Every Tuesday they played their favorite video game together, *Night of the Howling Moon*.

But today they were just eating sandwiches and pretending to do homework.

"Remember that year your mom surprised you with the giant cannoli from D'Amatos?" asked Charlotte as she leaned back away from the screen.

Marco laughed. "Yeah, we ate all the cream with giant spoons in your basement…"

"And then Jonah got sick and had to go puke it all up behind your garage!" Char almost fell off her chair laughing.

"Har har," said Jonah. He flicked a piece of eraser at her. "Remember the time we tried to have a sleepover and Char cried because she couldn't sleep without her brother in the room across the hall?"

"I was five!" Charlotte protested.

Marco looked back at Gio. "Whatever we do this year, it's gonna be unforgettable," he said. "We miss you, dude."

"Yeah, whatever you want, let us know and we'll make it happen," said Charlotte.

"Unless what you want is to beat the Cherufe,"

Jonah added. "We can't promise we'll figure that out in time."

For the past three Tuesdays, Gio and his friends had been trying to get past the Cherufe—half rock, half magma—that guarded the volcano in level 4 of *Night of the Howling Moon*. But the Cherufe burned them up every time.

"I don't know for sure," Gio said as he pulled a textbook out of his backpack. "But Mom definitely owes me. She's been asking for a lot of help with the dogs lately, so I figure I deserve a really *big* birthday surprise this year. And what's bigger than seeing you guys?"

For as long as Gio could remember, he'd spent his birthday with his friends from home. It was always just the four of them, and there was always chocolate cake with crushed potato chips on top.

But now he lived a seven-hour drive away. Too far for a day trip but not so far that he couldn't go home-home for a long weekend. Right?

He'd been dropping hints for weeks but his mom

just kept saying, "We'll see." And Gio's doggy spies hadn't turned up any intel. *Yet*.

Jonah looked up from his notebook. "Just because she owes you doesn't mean she'll do it."

Marco rolled his eyes. "You gotta have faith."

Just then, Gio heard a scratch at his door followed by whining.

Gio opened the door to find Bean sitting in the hallway with the stuffed dinosaur in his mouth. Its

tail had already been torn off. "Hey, how'd you get out of your crate?" Gio asked.

Bean dropped the dinosaur and sat up proudly. "Houdini taught me!"

Then he poked his head into Gio's room.

"Where did all the doggies go?" Bean asked.

Gio glanced at his clock. 6:30 pm. Their people must have already come to take them home.

"Are they in here?" Bean squiggled past Gio and bounded into his room.

"Hey, you can't just come in here," Gio said quietly. "No dogs allowed."

"Who are you talking to?" asked Jonah.

Gio froze. He glanced back at the computer screen. He hadn't even told his friends that he could talk to dogs yet. His new ability was kind of cool, but also kind of weird. Gio knew from movies that superpowers could make your life tricky. And his was already tricky enough!

Gio felt himself starting to sweat.

"Wait, is there a puppy in your room?" Charlotte

jumped out of her seat and ran over to the laptop they'd set up for the call.

"Yeah, we're fostering a chocolate Lab puppy," Gio said. He nudged Bean away from his backpack. "His name's Bean Burrito but we're calling him Bean."

"Let me see!" Charlotte squealed. "I wanna see that cute little fluffy floof!"

The speakers screeched and Gio covered his ears with his hands. Then Bean pawed at Char's face on the screen, and Gio's computer tipped backwards.

"Bean, no!" said Gio. But the word *no* didn't mean much to Bean yet.

Gio pulled the wriggly pup onto the ground and whispered in his ear, "You'll break it, and computers are expensive."

"But there are people in the box!" Bean said.

"They're not really here," Gio tried to explain without moving his lips. *If only they really were here.*

Bean squirmed out of Gio's arms and started stalking dust bunnies.

"He's not ours," Gio told his friends onscreen.

"We're just taking care of him until the shelter finds him a family."

"Is my family lost?" Bean asked, suddenly sad. He poked his head into the closet.

Gio shook his head. How could he even explain?

"Hey there, little guy!" Marco said. "Yo, that puppy is a keeper!"

"He's okay," said Jonah. Jonah was a cat person. And the only one of them with an actual pet.

"Labs are really great family dogs," said Marco. "They're mostly happy and they get along well with kids." Marco really wanted a dog a few years back, so he did all his school projects on different breeds. Then his twin brothers came along and his house got too chaotic for a pet.

Bean crawled out from under the bed with something in his mouth. It was Gio's limited edition *Night of the Howling Moon* werewolf action figure, and the pup was ready to chomp.

"Leave it!" Gio yelled. Then he whispered, "Trust me, that action figure is *not* gonna feel good coming out."

Bean paused, startled. Then he shook himself out and crouched back down into his hunting stance.

"No, wait!" Gio ripped off a piece of turkey from his sandwich and lured Bean away from the werewolf. When the puppy turned to gobble it up, Gio grabbed his action figure and pressed it close to his chest.

"See? When you 'leave it,' you get something better," he whispered.

In the background, he heard Charlotte's mom calling down the basement stairs.

"Are you all doing homework down there or are you gossiping with Gio? Hi Gio!"

Gio felt his shoulders relax. It was like he was right back where he belonged.

"Hi Helene!" he called.

Charlotte turned back to the screen. "We better go. That's her second warning. But don't worry. Your mom is gonna send you back to us for your birthday for sure!"

"We can't wait to see you!" said Marco. He fist-bumped the computer screen before turning back to his notebook.

"Don't let that dog destroy anything good," said Jonah.

Gio's computer screen went dark, and suddenly his room felt too quiet. He turned around to find Bean curled up on his bed surrounded by the stuffing from his favorite pillow.

"Can I sleep in here?" Bean asked.

Gio knew the puppy wasn't his forever. Would he get too attached if he slept on his bed?

"Mom has a whole crate set up for you downstairs, buddy," Gio said. "Like your own private bedroom."

"Why?" asked Bean.

Gio scratched the back of his head. "Um, well... Because she knows about dogs and what they need for sleeping? I don't know. I'm sure there's a good reason."

"But I miss my brothers and sisters," Bean whined.

Bean looked up at Gio with big, sad eyes and Gio felt his heart melting. He tried to think of something to say that would make Bean feel better, but he could only think of things that might make him feel worse.

It must be really hard to live with all your siblings one day and then be all on your own the next.

It was kind of like being with all your friends one day, and then in a new town the very next morning.

So Gio curled a blanket into a little nest around the puppy so he wouldn't get cold in the night. When Bean had settled in, Gio lay down next to him on the bed.

"I'll keep you safe," Gio whispered. "I promise."

CHAPTER FIVE

Dreams

The next morning, Gio woke up to an empty bed.

Uh-oh! Where's Bean? He sprang up with a fright.

If he'd lost the puppy on his first night in their house, his mom was going to ground him until dogs started flying. Then he'd *never* get to see his friends for his birthday!

Gio pulled on his clothes and raced downstairs.

Luckily, Bean was in the kitchen—*phew*! But he was with Gio's mom....

She was using bits of Bean's food as rewards to practice commands such as sit, down, touch, and high-five.

Bean jumped up and down. "Guess what, Gio?" he said. "I got blueberries with my breakfast!"

Gio ran a hand through his wavy hair. He was glad Bean was safe, but he had a feeling his mom was going to be mad.

"Sit," said Gio's mom.

Gio quickly sat down but then realized she was talking to the puppy.

Bean sat and held open his mouth for a blueberry. His brown tail thumped against the tiles. "I like blueberries!" he announced.

Gio hopped up and grabbed a cereal bar from the cabinet. "I'm going to bike over to the park to see if any of the guys from soccer are playing pickup," he told his mom.

But that wasn't happening.

"Have a seat, Gio," his mom said in her firm, there's-going-to-be-trouble voice.

Uh-oh. Gio's heart sank. He sat down and tried to look innocent.

"You know the dogs aren't allowed upstairs," she said.

Gio dropped his head onto the counter. "I didn't bring him upstairs. He just barged into my room," he explained.

"And you didn't bring him back down," his mom said. "Bean needs to sleep in his crate. It's how we keep him safe and avoid accidents."

She probably found him in my room and put him

in his crate herself . . . Gio thought. *Which is her actual job* . . .

His mom tossed a blueberry across the room for Bean to find. The puppy's oversized paws slipped on the tile floor as he ran after it.

Gio tried to keep his face blank. "I felt so bad for him and—"

"Dogs need structure, Gio," his mom said firmly. "We have to be clear about the rules so he'll grow up to be happy and well-trained."

Gio's eyebrows scrunched together. He still wasn't sure this was a punishable offense.

"Speaking of well-trained," she said. "I'll need your help socializing Bean today."

"What? I was going to play soccer!" Gio complained.

Bean was *her* project, but she wanted *him* to do all the work.

On the other hand . . . if he helped his mom, she'd have to give him what he wanted for his birthday. Right?

Then the doorbell rang and Bean bolted for the front door.

"It's Millie! I can smell her! Millie's here!" Bean barked.

Millie? Gio thought. *On a Saturday?* He heard her high-pitched voice calling for him from outside.

"Gioooo!" she howled. "Are you home? I brought Isa!"

Gio glanced back toward the kitchen where his mom was doing the dishes.

"Give me a sec," he told Isa—*and Millie*—through the door. "I can't open the door until Bean stops barking."

To Bean, he said "Sit" like his mom would want him to.

Bean couldn't control himself, though. "Open up, Gio! Millie came to play!" He leaped at the door like he was on a trampoline.

"I can't do it until you sit," Gio said quietly. Louder he said, "Bean, *sit*."

Bean touched his tail to the ground and Gio tossed him one of the store-bought treats his mom kept in

jars all over the house. But as soon as Gio's hand got close to the doorknob, Bean was up and barking again. Gio rolled his eyes.

"Just do it for two seconds so I can open the door, then you can do whatever you want," he whispered. "That's how this works."

Bean tilted his head. "Oh, okay," he said. He sat and gobbled more treats while Gio opened the door for his friends.

"We left squeaky banana here yesterday," Millie said as she rushed inside. She jumped up onto the couch and sniffed under the pillows. "You didn't let that puppy play with my banana, did you?" She leaped off the couch and stuck her nose under the green chair.

Gio knew the banana was upstairs in his backpack, but he couldn't tell Millie in front of Isa.

"It's okay, Millie," he said instead. He reached out to pet her. "Are you looking for your squeaky banana?"

"Ohhhh, *that's* why she dragged me here!" Isa said. "How do you always know exactly what Millie wants? It's like you can read her mind."

Isa squatted down and scratched behind Millie's ears while Millie glared at Gio.

"Just give her a lamb lung treat so I can talk to her," Millie said in *her* firm, there's-going-to-be-trouble voice. "And tell me where my banana is!"

She wriggled away and started sniffing around the living room again. Bean followed her.

"Guess what, Millie?" Bean said. "I had blueberries for breakfast. Wanna play tug?"

Things were already chaotic, and then Gio's mom walked into the room. "Isa! I'm glad you're here," she said. "I need Gio's help training Bean today, but no reason a friend can't go along on an outing."

Gio wanted to melt into the floor. He didn't really know Isa well enough for this. His mom barely knew Isa, either!

But Isa was in. "That sounds like so much fun! What do we have to do?"

Millie pawed at Gio's leg. "Can't we hang out?" she asked him.

But Gio's mom couldn't hear Millie's words.

"Great!" she said. "Bean needs to get used to being around people in all sorts of situations. I'm thinking you two can take him to the home goods store. Every time he notices something without barking, pulling, or jumping, give him a treat."

"Can I come, too?" Millie whined. She sat back and scratched behind her ears like she always did when she was nervous.

Gio sighed. He couldn't make everyone happy at once.

"How about we just go to the dog park?" he asked his mom. Millie would love that.

"Bean Burrito doesn't have all his shots yet, so he can't be around other dogs or their poop," she said. "The daycare dogs are safe because they have all their vaccines. . . ."

Gio felt his cheeks get warm. Did she have to talk about poop in front of Isa?

But Isa didn't notice. She was already sitting on the ground playing with Bean.

"Don't touch my person!" Millie snarled.

Bean pressed his body closer to Isa.

"Maybe it's better if we don't take Millie with us," Isa told Gio. "She can get a little jealous."

Millie barked, but only Gio knew that she was saying, "What? No! I want to hang out!"

Gio's mom made a suggestion she probably thought was helpful. "How about you just leave Millie here with me? I'll drop her off at Isa's house on my way to the store."

Millie's legs and tail went stiff. You didn't need to talk to dogs to know she was mad.

Gio leaned really close to Millie's ear and whispered, "You can see if she says anything about my birthday surprise. That's an important job." After all, Millie loved having a job to do.

But there was no fooling Millie. She pushed Gio away with her paws. "Gio, tell them I'll be good. Please don't have fun without me!"

"It's okay, Mom. We'll just keep Millie and Bean away from each other," he said. But he didn't feel so sure.

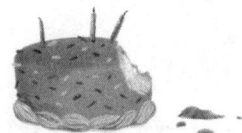

"It's no trouble at all," said Gio's mom. "Here, you two take this pouch of treats. Millie and I can play in the yard for a little while."

But Gio took one look at Millie and knew there was going to be trouble.

Double dog trouble.

CHAPTER SIX

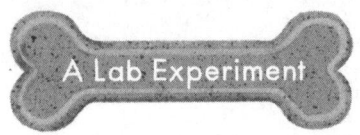
A Lab Experiment

Bean watched a girl with blue hair walk by and didn't make a peep, so Gio gave him a treat.

Bean noticed another person hurry past them. "That one looks grumpy!" Bean said without barking. Gio gave him another treat.

It was still morning, but Gio and Isa had decided the ice cream shop on Main Street was a much better place to socialize Bean than a store full of pillows and dishes.

They sat at a table out front where Bean could watch the people go by. They were careful to keep him on the bench next to Gio so he didn't try to play with other dogs.

"I think it's okay to have ice cream before noon

if it tastes like breakfast," Isa said as she handed Gio his cone.

Gio smiled and agreed. His ice cream was mocha-flavored and Isa's was matcha. He hadn't hung out with her outside school very much, but so far Isa had some great ideas.

"So what's the plan?" she asked. "We just hang out here and reward Bean every time he notices something and doesn't bark, jump, or try to tear it apart with his teeth? And this will teach him not to be afraid of the world?" she asked.

"That's what my mom said."

"Cool!" said Isa. "It's like we're shaping the future life of this little puppy. Getting him ready to find people who will love him." She licked the sprinkles off her ice cream.

He already has people who love him, Gio thought. Then he shook the thought out of his head. He wasn't Bean's people. He already had a house full of dogs.

"Can I try that?" Bean asked. He leaned his nose toward Gio's ice cream cone.

"No," said Gio as he blocked Bean with his elbow. Chocolate and coffee were *really* bad for dogs.

Bean yipped.

A man with a shaggy beard walked by. "That guy

has a hairy face," Bean said. It was rude, but he didn't stand up or bark, so Gio gave him another treat. Also, no one but Gio could hear what Bean said.

"I wish I'd known about socialization when Millie was a puppy," Isa went on. "Then maybe she wouldn't be afraid of big dogs or fireworks or clowns."

"Everyone is afraid of clowns," Gio said.

"Truth," said Isa. "And gym teachers."

Gio snorted and a glob of mocha fell off his cone onto the ground.

He felt a little guilty. Millie would have loved hanging out like this.

Bean hopped off the bench to sniff at the fallen ice cream.

"Leave it!" Gio said. Bean looked up for a second, but the ice cream smelled so good. He leaned back down to lick it.

"No, wait!" Gio kneeled down beside Bean and spoke in a low voice so Isa couldn't hear.

"Remember, if I say 'leave it' and you don't eat the thing, I'll give you a better treat—just like last night."

"Ooh, did you bring turkey?" Bean asked, his tail wagging.

Gio pulled a ziplock bag full of turkey out of his pocket and showed Bean.

"Ohboyohboyohboy!" said Bean. He sat back and his whole body shook, but he didn't bark, so Gio gave him some turkey.

"Good boy!" Gio told Bean.

"I AM a good boy!" said Bean. "And smart, too!" He hopped back up onto the bench next to Gio. Isa and Gio quickly cleaned up the messy ice cream.

"I didn't think you could reason with a puppy like that," Isa said.

If you only knew, Gio thought. But maybe he *was* really good at this whole dog-training thing.

"Omigosh, your dog is so cute! Can we come say hi?" a teenager with a corgi squealed at Gio and Bean from across the street.

"Ooh, a friend!" Before Gio knew what was happening, Bean jumped off the bench and darted away. Isa grabbed for his leash but it slipped through her fingers.

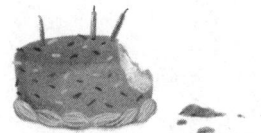

"Bean, no!" Gio shouted.

But the corgi was also shouting, "Hey, little buddy, come smell *this*!" And that sounded like way more fun to Bean. So the pup bounded toward the street.

Gio's heart froze. There was so much traffic on Main Street. Okay, right now it was stopped at a red light, but in a minute it would be moving fast. Gio ran toward Bean and tried to grab him.

"Ooh, fun, is this a game? Can't catch me!" Bean said. He darted out into the road.

"You gotta run away from him," Isa called to Gio. "So he'll chase you."

"What?" Gio was fully panicking. *How can I do that?*

The light changed, and an SUV came around the corner.

Gio took a deep breath and a few steps backwards.

"Try to get me!" he called to Bean shakily. *I sure hope this works!*

Bean bounced toward Gio but the SUV was getting closer.

"Bean, quick, come here!" Gio yelled. He didn't know what to do. If he ran toward Bean, the puppy would dart farther into the street. But if he didn't—

CHAPTER SEVEN

Before Gio could make his next move, a boy on a bike scooped Bean up, then jumped the curb and skidded to a stop in front of Gio and Isa.

Bean licked the boy's face. "This one smells like farts!" he said.

"Gabe?" Gio couldn't believe Milton's biggest bully had just *saved* Bean's life.

Gabe Farber was tall and lanky with wavy hair and a mean smile. He was on Gio's soccer team but he never passed Gio the ball. Instead, he howled at him and called him names like Dog Breath and New Kid.

One time, he'd spotted Gio talking to Millie in public. *That* wasn't fun!

"Gotta teach your dog some manners, New Kid," Gabe sneered.

Gio practically growled. "Stuff it, Gabe," he snapped. He knew he wasn't supposed to let bullies know they bothered him, but this was about Bean.

Isa gently took Bean from Gabe's arms and snuggled him close.

"Bean, you can't do that," Gio said. "You scared us!" He didn't care who heard him say it.

Gabe rolled his eyes. "You know what your problem is, *Barker*? You're too soft. On the soccer field and with this dog. You have to show him you're in charge. Teach him what a real pack leader is like."

Gabe clapped his hands so loud, Bean flinched and buried his head in Isa's shoulder.

"No way," said Gio. "It doesn't work like that. You can't scare a dog into doing what you want." Maybe he wasn't a master trainer yet, but he knew that much.

"Says the kid who let his dog run out into the street." Gabe said. "Looks like your game is off, Dog Breath."

"You're all bark and no bite, Gabriel," Isa said.

She gently placed Bean on the ground, making sure she had a firm grip on his leash.

Gabe pretended he didn't hear her. Instead, he looked down at Bean and raised an eyebrow. Then a corner of his mouth ticked up into a smirk.

"Hey, isn't this one of the Lab puppies up for adoption at the shelter?" Gabe said. "I was there with my dad. We've been looking for a rescue . . ."

Gabe snapped his fingers to get Bean to jump.

"Woo woo woo!" Bean barked and leaped toward Gabe's fingers.

When he caught the corner of Gabe's shirt

between his teeth, Gabe nudged him away with his knee and a little too much force.

Bean ducked behind Gio's leg.

"Giooo, I don't like this kid!" he whined.

"Leave him alone, Gabe," Gio said. It was one thing to mess with Gio. But Bean couldn't even defend himself.

"Whatever," Gabe said. "See you at your doghouse, BarkBarkBarker. When I come to pick up my new puppy." Gabe hopped back on his bike and sped away.

Gio took a deep breath. Bean was safe from cars, but now he was in a worse kind of danger.

"We can*not* let that bully adopt Bean," he told Isa. He paced back and forth on the sidewalk.

"Just because Gabe wants to adopt Bean doesn't mean his parents will let him," Isa said calmly.

"What's a bully?" Bean asked, his voice quavering. "What's adopt?"

"I promised Bean I'd take care of him," Gio told Isa. "He trusts me!"

Bean pawed at Gio's jeans. "Is a bully like a meanie?" he asked quietly. "Is it like Houdini?"

Gio felt his heart racing. What good was being able to talk to dogs if he couldn't use his power to help Bean?

Isa said, "Well, let's focus on what we can do. Can we find Bean a better home before Gabe has time to do anything?"

Bean curled his body into Gio's legs. "I have a home," Bean said. "It's Gio's home."

"I know, buddy," Gio said. He didn't want Bean to leave Barker's Doghouse yet, either.

Could he get his mom to talk to the people at the shelter? She hated that pack-leader training style.

"Wait, I'm getting an idea!" said Isa. She bounced up and down on her toes. "There's a sign up at the daycare, right? Something about an open house at Barker's Doghouse?"

"Yeah, something like that," Gio said. His mom was doing it to get more clients. But he'd tuned out the details.

"So, a bunch of people who love dogs are going to be in your house, right?" Isa said.

"I guess so." Gio imagined a bunch of strangers in his house and his stomach started to hurt. This wasn't helping.

"Well, who says we can't have our own plan for the open house?" Isa pushed on. She started pacing, too—but not in a worried way like Gio. She was inspired.

"How about this? Evie and I will talk to the people at the shelter. We'll find out if anyone amazing is looking to adopt a puppy. Then we'll invite *those* people to the open house, too. Once they're at Barker's Doghouse, they'll meet Bean and fall in love!" She squatted down and rubbed Bean's chin.

"Everyone loves me!" Bean said proudly.

Gio was starting to understand what she was saying. "So, Gabe won't be able to adopt Bean because we'll have already found him the perfect home. . . ."

Bean barked his approval.

"We're brilliant!" said Isa. "You focus on training Bean. And let me and Evie handle the rest."

And with my superpower, Gio thought, *I'll train Bean to be the best puppy ever.*

Isa held out her fist for a bump. "Let our secret mission begin!"

CHAPTER EIGHT

When Gio got home from school on Monday, Bean was wandering around the backyard with his head stuck inside a stuffed volcano.

The volcano had come packed with little squeaky dinosaurs for the dogs to pull out. Bean's head must have been small enough to fit inside but too big to remove.

Every so often, Avocado half-heartedly tugged at the volcano with his teeth and said things like, "Put some muscle into it, Sport" or "Must be snuggly in there."

Gio's mom's assistant, Janice, was sitting on the back stoop editing YouTube videos on her laptop as usual. She wore giant headphones and sang off-key to some pop song Gio kind of recognized.

She wasn't stepping in to help the puppy. She didn't even notice what was going on.

At the far end of the yard, Millie and Gary played tug with a rope toy.

It's kind of weird that Millie didn't run over to say hi, Gio thought. She wasn't helping Bean, either.

Gio watched as Bean hobbled toward the big tree. He bopped it gently with his head and stood there like he didn't know what to do next.

"This is not cool," Gio said to the dogs in the yard. "Get Bean out of there right now."

"Little Beano is safe in there," said Avocado.

"And we're safe from his chompers," added Houdini.

"Hi Gio!" Bean called. He did a little dance and tried to shake the volcano off his head but it didn't work.

"Now," Gio demanded.

"On it!" sang Avocado. He ran over to Bean and bit down on the top of the volcano.

"Hold still, little Bean," said Avocado. "Now, pull backwards on three."

Bean braced his front paws.

"One, two, three!" Avocado yanked off the volcano and Bean went flying into Gio. Both of them landed with a thud on the grass.

Millie and Gary leaped over Gio's stomach and kept running.

Is Millie ignoring me? Gio wondered.

"That was fun!" said Bean. "Gotta run!"

He chased after Millie and Gary shouting, "Hey, wait for me!" But the other dogs acted like they didn't even hear the pup.

Gio hated to see them leaving Bean out of their games. He'd felt like the odd man out at soccer practice for so long. He knew how hard it was to make new friends. It stank!

"Come on, Bean, let's go inside," he said.

But Millie ran in front of Gio to block his path. She barked once and planted her paws in the grass.

"Oh, Bean's allowed in your room now, huh? What are you, besties? Are you going to give his new owner treats so *they* can talk to each other?"

For a moment, Gio wished he couldn't talk to the dogs at all.

What was he supposed to say? Bean was a puppy. He needed Gio. Being friends with Bean didn't mean he wasn't friends with Millie anymore.

But how could he explain that to a schnoodle?

Meanwhile, Bean followed his nose to the stairs where Gio had dropped his backpack. He sniffed at the pockets, then stuck his snout inside the front flap. He pulled out something rubbery and yellow.

"Look!" said Bean. "It's a banana! But not a

banana for eating. It's a banana for squeaking!" He pressed the toy between his sharp teeth.

"Bean, no," said Gio. "Leave it!"

Millie froze and her tail went stiff.

"That's *my* squeaky banana!" she yelled from across the yard.

Bean tossed the banana high up in the air. When it dropped back down, he caught it in his mouth.

Millie charged at Bean. The puppy dodged her and circled the treehouse.

"Oh, this is going to be good," said Houdini. She stopped digging and lay down in front of the tree for a better view.

"Keep away from *my* banana!" Millie ordered. She tried to tackle Bean while Gary came at him from the other direction.

Gary was fast, but Bean was already bigger.

"You wanna play keep-away?" said Bean. "Can't catch me!" In a flash, he was past the other dogs again.

"Little dog's on the run!" Avocado sang. He gave Bean a hard stare and tried to block his path, but Bean

darted between his legs and under the back deck.

"You come out of there right now," Millie growled.

Gio heard loud chomping and tearing noises from under the deck—the kind his great-uncle Herc made every year at Thanksgiving dinner.

Millie whimpered. "He's killing it!" she whined. "Gio, do something!"

"Here, Bean," Gio said while patting the ground in front of the porch. "Come on out!" But Bean just scooched farther back under the deck.

"Bean, remember 'leave it'?" Gio said. "If you give me the banana, I'll give you something even better." That did the trick. Treats *always* did the trick. But when Bean sat down next to Gio, a rubbery yellow triangle was stuck to his tongue.

Millie stomped over to Bean and shoved her face in his.

Gio knew that was a sign of aggression, so he stepped between the dogs. But he didn't know what else to do.

"You killed my banana!" Millie growled. "We are *SO* not going to be friends!"

"He didn't mean it, Millie," Gio said. "He's just a puppy."

"You stay out of it! This is dog business," Millie snapped. "You took Bean on a field trip and left me behind. And you let him destroy my squeaky banana!"

"Bean has to be socialized," Gio said. "He has to learn how to be out in the world."

"But you went with my person, Gio! You know how much I love hanging out with you and Isa!"

Houdini shoved Millie and Gary out of her way. "Cut to the chase," she said. "Just give the schnoodle what she wants, Giovanni David Barker. Or we're going to chew up all your sneakers."

Gio couldn't believe the dogs were ganging up on him like this.

"Millie's been a loyal friend," Gary explained calmly. "She deserves the chance to see if the treats your mom makes will help her talk to Isa."

"I've been spying for you and everything!" Millie wailed.

Yeah, not that you found anything out, Gio thought.

"And what do I get in return?" Millie asked. "Left behind!" She pressed her side against Gary's.

Gio took a deep breath.

"I gotta get out of here," he said. "Let's go, Bean." Gio grabbed his backpack and stomped toward the back door, with Bean padding up the stairs behind him.

The dogs were his pack. They were the best friends he had here in Milton. And he felt like he had just lost them.

CHAPTER NINE

Falling Apart

"Let's do this," Jonah said as his griffon avatar popped onto the screen. "My mom is making me go to my aunt's house in an hour. And I'd really feel better about it if we kicked some magma butt first."

"You got it," said Marco. His ogre pumped a fist into the air.

"Take that, Rock Monster!" CharChar cried out.

On the computer screen, her dragon avatar breathed fire at the giant Cherufe. The Cherufe looked human but it was made out of rock and magma so the fire made it double in size.

They were trying to get past the volcanoes in level four—but it wasn't going well.

Gio was so thrown by the fight with Millie that he

called an emergency gaming session. But he still felt frustrated because he couldn't tell his friends what was really going on.

It was a lot!

He was trying to train a puppy to impress his mom so she'd let him visit his friends for his birthday.

He was trying to keep that same puppy out of a bully's hands.

And he, a human, was in the middle of a dog fight for reasons that were getting harder and harder to explain to his human friends who were way too far away.

Bean rested quietly on the bed while Gio played.

Gio felt a little better knowing that by the time the game was over, the rest of the dogs would already be home.

Onscreen, the Cherufe reached up and grabbed Char's dragon by the wing. It opened its jagged, rocky mouth like it was going to swallow her whole.

"No way, dude!" Gio shouted.

Gio's werewolf and Marco's ogre ran at the

Cherufe while Jonah's griffon attacked from the air. The Cherufe tossed Char's dragon into the others and knocked them over like bowling pins.

Then it blasted them with its fiery breath.

Game over. Again. But Gio didn't care. He was too busy thinking about Millie's demands. She wanted him to give treats to Isa so they could talk to one another. But wasn't that blackmail?

And seriously . . . what if the rest of the dogs started wanting treats for their humans? Did Gio really want all those other people talking to his dog friends? A part of him really liked having them to himself.

On the screen, his werewolf tripped over a small pika rabbit and stumbled, almost falling into a lava pit.

"You okay over there, Gio?" Char asked.

Gio paused the game.

Marco and Charlotte popped onto the screen. Char was lying on the floor with her feet up on the sofa. Marco stood up to stretch.

"Okay, I have a question," Gio told his friends.

"Go for it," said Marco just as Jonah came into view carrying a bag of tortilla chips and a bowl of guacamole.

"What if you had a magical power . . . ?" said Gio. "No one else has it and no one knows you have it. Do you share it with anyone?"

"Ooh, What-Ifs," said Jonah as he sat down on the arm of the sofa. "I love this game!"

"I need more details," said Char, holding up a chip. "Is it a magical power in real life or in the game? Can it help us defeat the Cherufe?"

"Um, yeah," said Gio. "What if your character could talk to the Cherufe? Or something like that. Find out what it wanted."

"That would be cool," said Jonah. "But it depends on who you want to share the power with."

"Us?" asked Char. "Then, yes, one hundred percent, no question. Just do it."

"What if it's somebody I just met?" Gio asked. Out of the corner of his eye, Gio saw Bean crawl out from under his desk.

"You have to figure out if you can trust them first," said Marco.

"Yeah," said Jonah. "Like would they use the magic for good or evil?"

Gio thought about it for a second. He remembered the way Isa had volunteered to help him find Bean a good family. And the way she'd suggested eating ice cream for breakfast.

"Good I think," he said. He paused for a second. "But what if you kind of wanted to be the only one who had the magic?"

"Sounds selfish not to share," said Char. She scooped up some guac with a chip and ate it in one bite.

"No, it doesn't," said Jonah. "You don't have to share if you don't want to." He picked up his controller, ready to restart the game.

"But why not make someone else's life better if you could?" asked Marco.

Gio's head started to hurt. He didn't want to keep secrets anymore. He wanted to tell his friends what was really going on. But would they be mad when they found out he hadn't told them about something as big as a superpower? Would they even *want* to see him on his birthday?

"Guys, there's something I have to tell you. It's

big and you're not going to believe it. But it's one hundred percent true."

"Spill it, then let's spill this lava monster's guts," Jonah said.

"Okay, well, I can—"

The doorbell rang, and Bean started barking and darted at the door. He had a big voice for a small puppy.

Gio's mom called up the stairs. "Gio, your friend's here!"

He glanced back at his computer screen. His friends were already here.

The bedroom door opened and suddenly Isa was standing *in his room* holding a stack of papers.

She bent down to greet Bean.

"Hello BeanieBeanBean," she said.

Gio quickly looked around for anything embarrassing like underwear or babyish toys. He kicked a balled-up werewolf sock under the bed and stood up awkwardly.

"Relax," said Isa. "I'm not here to judge. I have

the fliers for the open house. I wanted to show them to you before I hang them up all over town." Then she spotted his computer screen. "Oh, are those your friends from home? Hi Gio's friends!" She waved and they all waved back.

"Um, we're—" Gio took some of the fliers. Isa sat down next to Bean and kept talking.

"Evie and I have already stopped by the shelter to see if they have any families interested in adopting the cutest chocolate Lab ever. The answer is *yes!* And they gave us a whole list of names. So we're going to put a flier in each of their mailboxes."

She scratched Bean behind the ears. "There's no way Bean is going to go home with Gabe. We're going to find Bean an excellent family at the open house."

Bean whined when he heard the word *family*.

But Gio was staring at something on the fliers.

"This says Friday the tenth," he said.

Isa looked up, confused. "Yeah, this Friday. That's the date your mom told me."

"But Friday the tenth is my birthday," he said.

"It's your birthday?!" Isa said, excited. "Why didn't you tell me?"

"Whoa, whoa, whoa," Jonah said. "Your mom planned an open house for the daycare on your *birthday?*"

"It's okay," Gio said as the news sunk in. "I don't have to go to the open house. I can still come see you guys for my birthday. Mom doesn't need me."

He knew that wasn't right, but it *had* to be right. Right?

Gio felt like he was falling apart along with his birthday plans. He'd only wanted this one thing.

He saw Isa shrug at his friends. He wished she would just go home and take the fliers with her.

It's not like I'm *ever going to get to go home*, he thought.

"Hey, where's Bean?" Isa asked.

Suddenly, the computer screen went dark.

Gio switched it on and off. Nothing.

He looked under the desk.

Bean smiled up at him with his best I'm-so-cute face.

The little Lab had completely chewed through the cords.

CHAPTER TEN

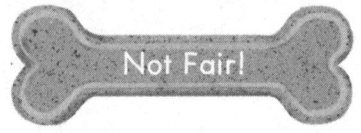

Gio stomped down the stairs, clenching the flier in his fist.

"Mom!" he called. "Mom!"

She was in the kitchen trying to teach Millie to roll over, but Millie just wanted to sneak upstairs.

"I'm right here, Gio, you don't have to yell," his mom said.

"It's not fair!" Millie huffed. "Why does Bean get to hang out in your room but I have to wait down here?"

"Not now," Gio told her. He didn't even care if his mom heard him.

His mom took in his body language—his stiff shoulders and shaking hands—and her face softened.

"Gio, what's wrong?" she asked. "Are you okay?" She tried to hug him but he shrugged her off.

"The open house. For the daycare. Is on my *birthday*? Are you kidding me?"

His mom looked surprised. "Gio, you knew that. I've been talking about the open house for weeks. That's the only day—"

"I haven't been listening! I thought you were going to surprise me with a trip home!" Gio said, annoyed.

Then, more softly, he said, "I want to go home for my birthday. I want to spend this one day with Marco and Jonah and CharChar like I always do. I thought you knew that." He wiped a tear off his cheek but more kept coming.

His mom looked at the floor. "I'm really sorry, Gio," she said. "It's already planned."

"I could still go," he answered. "It's not too late! You don't need me here for the open house. Isa can help and you have Janice."

His mom stifled a laugh at the mention of Janice.

Millie settled down between Gio and his mom, watching them both very carefully.

"I can take a ride share," Gio said. "Or the bus!"

Gio's mom sighed. "It's complicated. There's a lot going on here and money . . ." Her voice trailed off.

Gio groaned and leaned against the kitchen island. "Mom, if you are about to say money doesn't grow on trees . . ."

"I am very deliberately trying NOT to use those exact words," his mom said.

Gio looked at her. "So the money's not there?"

"It is not," she said. "That's why I'm hosting the open house. To get more clients. And I would love for you to show off what you've done with Bean. If more people hire us to train their dogs instead of just dog-sitting them, we can charge more and—"

Gio started to zone out again, but this time his mom noticed. Quickly, she changed the subject.

"How about we have a birthday party for you here?" she said. "I can bake a cake for the open house,

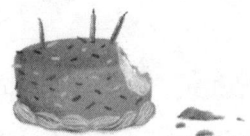

and you can invite Isa and your new friends from soccer." Her voice sounded so hopeful.

Isa. Gio wondered if she was still in his room. Had she noticed he still had bins of Legos?

"I don't want to share my birthday with Barker's Doghouse," he said firmly.

"Fair enough." His mom shifted closer to him. "But ya know, sometimes you have to let go of the way things have always been to make room for something even better to come along."

Gio scowled. "You can't just teach me to leave it, Mom. I'm not a *dog*."

She didn't try to stop him when he went outside to calm down on the porch swing.

After a few minutes, Millie came out and jumped onto the swing next to him. Gio scratched behind her ears without even thinking about it.

"It stinks that you can't spend your birthday with your friends," she said. Then she remembered that she was still mad at him and moved to the other end of the swing.

"You're still mad at me? What did I do?"

"You've been a crummy friend." Millie pouted. "Once Bean came along, you stopped hanging out with me."

"Crummy friend?" Gio stared at her for a long time. He tried to remember the last time he and Millie had gone for a walk or played fetch.

"I'm sorry, that is crummy," Gio said. "But Bean's a puppy. I have to teach him stuff. And we have to find him a home before Gabe adopts him."

Millie walked across the swing and pawed at Gio's knee. "Best friends do missions together."

That's true, Gio thought, *but*—

"Hey, *I'm* your best friend?" he asked.

Millie bopped him with her paw. "Of course, Gio! Isa's my person, Gary's my doggy bestie, and *you* are my best friend."

Gio smiled. "So you admit it's possible to have more than one very close friend . . ."

"Of course, but—oh." Millie looked away. "You think I should understand that you have enough love and friendship in your heart for me *and* Bean."

"I do." Gio pushed his feet against the floor to make the swing rock.

"You're still a stinker!" Millie planted her feet.

"What, me? Why?"

"Because I don't ignore you when Isa and Gary are around. I include you. And I don't let Isa eat your favorite squeaky toys." Millie was talking faster and faster.

Gio raised an eyebrow. Then he remembered how he'd panicked when he saw his favorite action figure in Bean's mouth. "You're right. I'm sorry I wasn't able to protect squeaky banana."

"Puppies are sneaky, Gio. I tried to warn you!" Millie was so worked up she was panting.

"They are. You're right," Gio said. "You told me how sharp Bean's teeth would be and I didn't understand until I saw the destruction for myself."

He scratched behind Millie's ears until she lay back down. "And I'm sorry I've been putting you off. The truth is, I like being the only kid who can talk to dogs. I didn't want to share that power with Isa. But I'm ready now. I'll ask Mom to bake some of those lamb lung treats for you. I don't want to be the person who keeps your dream from coming true."

"Really?" Millie jumped up and spun around. Then she licked Gio's cheek. The swing shook. "Oh, Gio, it's going to be so much fun!"

She settled down and rested her chin on his knee.

"I wish your mom felt that way about your birthday surprise."

"Me too," he said.

"It's not fair that you might have to see Gabe on your birthday."

"It's not fair that you can't talk to Isa—*yet*," Gio said.

"And it's not fair that Bean gets all the attention just 'cause he's little and dangerous," Millie noted.

She hopped down off the swing and shook herself out. "Okay, I feel better now. I'm so glad we're friends again!"

"That's it? You're not mad anymore?" Gio was surprised but glad.

"Of course not!" Millie said. "It doesn't feel good to be mad." Millie started humming as she pulled a stuffed llama out of the toy bin.

Millie shook the toy from side to side, then dropped it. "Thing is, Gio. All that stuff? It really *isn't* fair. But what are you going to do? You can either be miserable on the biggest day of your year or you can howl it out, then . . ."

Gio smirked. "Let me guess, I can let it go?"

"Yes! And you might end up having a different kind of fun. Maybe not. But at least there's a chance."

"Now you really sound like my mom."

"Well, she did train me a little," Millie said as she carried the stuffed llama back to the bin. "I'd better go find Isa. She's probably snooping in your closet."

CHAPTER ELEVEN

Countdown

The rest of the school week passed by in a fog. Gio's computer was still broken, so he missed gaming with his friends, but they did a homework hang over the phone instead.

By the time his birthday rolled around, he felt a little calmer. He was trying *really* hard to look on the bright side. He had a puppy to train and a secret mission to find a forever family for that puppy at the open house.

Isa and Evie had invited some great families to come and meet Bean. They'd also put fliers up all over school and Main Street—just in case. They were determined to make sure Bean went to an awesome forever home.

And so was Gio. He still hadn't guessed his

birthday surprise, but he already knew it wasn't what he wanted . . . so he was trying really, *really* hard to let it go—just like Millie had suggested.

But the truth was, looking on the bright side made him want to nap.

I can do this! Gio thought as he walked into Barker's Doghouse after school that day.

He could hear his mom upstairs, and the house smelled like peanut butter. *Good sign*, Gio thought. *That means Mom baked the dog treats.*

He'd be sure to save one for Isa. Maybe she'd be talking to Millie by the end of the party!

When he got inside, Moose, the Great Dane, was lying in his regular spot behind the front door. He raised his head for a chin rub and drooled all over Gio's hand. It was gross—but also comforting. At least one thing never changed.

As soon as Gio stepped into the living room Millie, Gary, Houdini, and Avocado launched themselves at him. Gio plopped down on the floor. Then they licked his face until he made them stop. "Happy birthday, Gio!" the dogs cheered.

"We're sorry we couldn't find anything out about your mom's surprise!" Avocado said.

"But *we* have a surprise for you!" Millie added.

"It's kind of like a birthday present," Gary said.

"Except we're dogs, so it's not like we bought it or wrapped it or anything," Millie chimed in.

A buzz of excitement was building inside Barker's Doghouse and Gio was starting to feel it, too. The living room/dining room was already clean and ready for guests.

The toys and chews were all tucked away in clearly labeled bins along the wall. Pamphlets, jars of treats, and pictures of the dogs doing tricks sat on every surface and human snacks were set up on the dining room table.

His mom had been drilling the dogs all week. Their job was to show the people at the open house how well-behaved and happy they were at the daycare. That way, everyone would want to send their dogs to Barker's Doghouse, too!

"Let's go! Let's go! Let's go!" Millie tugged at him to stand up.

"It's surprise time!" Avocado herded him past the table toward the kitchen. Gio dug a chip into a pile of guac on his way out. *His* manners didn't have to be as good as the dogs', right?

"Where are the rest of the pups?" he asked. He couldn't see Bean anywhere. Was the puppy with his mom, or Janice?

"We haven't seen Felix in days and Houdini is coming back later with her person," Gary told him as they stepped through the back door and into the yard.

The backyard was also set up for the open house, with the dogs' balls and outdoor toys clean and on display.

Janice was in her usual spot under the tree, with her head buried in her phone, probably doing last-minute social media posts for the open house.

And there was Bean! He was sitting up in a mini treehouse wearing a polka-dotted bow tie and his tail drummed against the wood.

"Hi Gio!" Bean called. He raised a paw in the puppy version of a wave.

Avocado ducked underneath the deck, and suddenly peppy music blasted through the yard.

"Whoa! What's happening here?" Janice jumped up and almost jabbed herself on a tree branch.

Gio shrugged. For once, he had no idea.

"You're up to something," Janice said. Then she headed back into the house. "I don't want to get blamed for this. I'll be in your room live streaming. Call me when your mom's back."

"You can't hang out in my room. You don't live here. You *work* here." Janice just waved her hand at him and kept walking.

Millie tugged at his pants and Gio sat down in the grass.

"Ready?" Avocado asked. "Hit it!"

Bean leaped off the platform and launched into a routine of amazing tricks.

"Figure eight, jump, jump, twist!" Millie called out. Bean ran around in a figure eight, jumped twice over the plastic fire hydrant, and finished with a twist in the air.

"Catch, fetch, sit!" called Gary as Avocado catapulted a ball across the yard.

Bean dashed to catch it in his mouth. Then he brought it over to Gio, placed it at his feet, and sat like an angel, panting and out of breath.

"Time for the grand finale, Beano!" Avocado called. He slammed his paw down on a squeaky toy—his way of whistling—and Bean ran at the big tree.

Gio's body tensed. "No, wait, what are you doing?!"

"I got this!" said Bean. He pushed off the tree with his front paws and did a backflip onto Gio's old skateboard. It rolled a few feet across the grass. Then Bean hopped off and took a doggy bow.

The other dogs howled, hooted, and barked.

"Whoa!" said Gio. "When did you learn all that?" He couldn't believe they'd taught Bean so many tricks! And they weren't leaving him out anymore!

"Gio, I'm part of the pack!" Bean shouted. "I'm really part of the pack!" He ran at Gio and jumped up into his arms.

"You sure are, buddy," he said. He let Bean lick his face, then sat down with the puppy in his lap.

Gio felt tears prick at his eyes. He remembered

how bad Gabe had made him feel at school and at soccer practice. But then the dogs had taught him to dribble faster and improved his game. And now they were doing the same for Bean.

Gio got that feeling in his heart again—like he wanted to protect Bean from anything sad. He didn't want to have to say good-bye on his birthday.

Maybe whoever adopts Bean will send him to Barker's so we'll still get to see each other every day, Gio thought.

Millie rested her chin on Gio's knee. Avocado rested his on the top of Gio's head. And Gary squeezed onto his lap next to Bean so that they were all touching—like a big puppy pileup.

"We got this," said Avocado. The dogs all knew about the secret mission to find Bean a home away from Gabe, but no one wanted to make Bean anxious by talking about it. "We're here for you."

"And Isa will be here for you, too," said Millie. "Bullies don't mess with her."

Gio smiled. He scratched behind Millie's ear until her back leg started thumping.

This new life isn't all *bad*, he thought.

The doorbell rang and Gio looked back at the house. None of the dogs barked.

"This is it!" Millie said.

And they walked inside as a pack.

CHAPTER TWELVE

"Treats, please!" said Bean. All the dogs sat in a line in front of the counter waiting politely for their rewards.

Gio gave one of his mom's homemade treats to each dog. There was still a whole plateful left for Isa.

Gio winked at Millie. He'd asked his mom to bake them as a thank-you to the dogs for being on their best behavior. But Gio and Millie knew what they were really for.

Then Gary tugged at Millie's tail. "Last one to get a treat from a guest is a rotten egg!" he said, and the two dogs raced into the living room.

"Gotta run, Sport," Avocado said. "We've got a job to do!"

Gio could already hear lots of voices in the living

room. He tried to breathe through his jitters. He wanted to stay calm so Bean would feel calm—but it wasn't easy.

"What if nobody likes me?" Bean asked.

Gio kneeled down next to Bean. The puppy's tail was tucked and he looked a little shaky.

"You've got this," Gio whispered. "Let me know if you need to take a break. Remember, all you have to do is be yourself."

And Isa and I will find you the perfect family, he thought.

"*We* got this," said Bean, and he headed into the dining room.

Gio turned around to see his mom come down the stairs and pull a cake out of the refrigerator.

"Mom," said Gio, alarmed. "You promised this wouldn't be a birthday party."

"People have to eat," his mom said. "There aren't any candles. So it's just a cake."

Gio leaned over to get a better look.

"Chocolate with crushed potato chips on top

instead of frosting?" He raised an eyebrow. It was his favorite cake.

His mom shrugged. "Potato chips *with ridges*," she said. "It's a birthday tradition."

Not everything has to be different, Gio thought. He smiled. "I'll take it!"

"Do me a favor, grab that soda and follow me out?" she said.

Gio grabbed the drinks and followed his mom into the living room.

There were way more people there than he'd expected.

Most of them were couples, but there was a family with little kids, too, and a few people on their own. Some of them were people Gio recognized from town. Gio wondered which ones Isa and Evie had invited.

Janice was playing tour guide, live streaming the open house while showing potential clients where the dogs played, trained, and slept. One couple was very impressed by the bins of chew toys.

Isa was already there, carrying a clipboard. Bean

and Avocado were scoping out the scene from under the dining room table. Houdini had already arrived and was sitting on the couch with her person, chewing a bone like the most angelic dog on the planet.

A few minutes later, Evie walked in with a couple of guys from Gio's soccer team. Mason was holding a soccer ball and Rami and Harrison each had bags of gear with them.

Gio started to panic. *The guys from soccer are here?* he thought. But he looked behind Mason, and Gabe wasn't part of the group.

Gio felt himself relax a little.

"We were headed out for a pickup game, but then we heard it was your birthday, so we thought we'd see if you wanted to play," Mason said.

He *did* want to play, but . . .

Rami peered around Gio. He had spiky hair and played excellent defense. "Looks like you're having a party we weren't invited to?"

Gio felt his cheeks get hot.

"We're just messing with you," said Harrison. He gave Gio a pat on the shoulder. His freckles bunched up when he smiled. "We know it's an open house. There are fliers all over town."

Gio cringed as he watched them taking in the row of mats for the dogs and the gear for training. Part of him wished a lava crater would open up in his living room and swallow him whole.

But Rami turned to Gio with a big smile on his face. "It's so cool that this is your mom's job."

"Yeah," Harrison agreed. "My mom is an accountant."

"Hey, women who math are cool," Evie said. She elbowed him gently.

"Not my mom." Harrison took the ball from Mason and twirled it on his finger as if it were a basketball.

Gio felt Avocado walk up and sit beside him. "I can get a game set up in the backyard, Sport," Avocado suggested. "You can come out and play with us later!"

That could be fun! Gio smiled to himself. Avocado was born to be a coach.

"Um, if you want, you can kick the ball around in our backyard," he told his teammates. "We have snacks and I think I can come out later." Avocado thumped him with his tail.

"Oh, and, um, this is Avocado. He can show you where we keep the cones and stuff."

Avocado showed off his best sit and barked twice.

"Tell them I can coach, too," he said. "Your team's

offense wasn't connecting in your last playoff game. They need to work on their passing."

Gio tried really hard not to roll his eyes.

"Avocado can play, too, if you need a fourth," Gio added. "He's got some good soccer . . . um, *tricks*."

"So cool!" Rami said

"Well then, let's go, buddy." Mason scratched the top of Avocado's head.

Isa walked over with her clipboard and Millie hopped up onto the arm of the couch.

"This is going so well!" Millie and Isa said at the same time.

Gio smiled. "Yeah, I guess so."

It didn't feel weird to have some of the guys from his team here. It actually felt kind of good. And it would be great to get to play soccer on his birthday . . . But he still had a bad feeling and he couldn't figure out why.

He looked around the living room.

His mom was laughing with a few adults over by the fireplace.

Janice was trying to upsell a couple on a deluxe

daycare package including doggy massages and spa treatments. Where would his mom even put a spa?

Moose was in the same spot by the front door, making a puddle of drool on the tile.

Gabe was *not* in his house.

And Bean was . . .

Gio scanned the ground for a wagging brown tail. No Bean.

"Hey, where's Bean?" Gio asked.

Millie barked in alarm.

"Yikes!" she cried. "He's gonna eat the cake!"

CHAPTER THIRTEEN

No More Treats!

Bean was up on the dining room table, silently skulking toward Gio's birthday cake.

"Smells so good!" Bean said as he stepped in a bowl of dip.

Gio glanced at his mom. She was showing some potential clients the toys and treats she used for training on the other side of the room.

None of the adults had noticed Bean—*yet*. But there was *no way* they were going to be able to ignore a puppy trashing the snack table.

"Bean, no, that's chocolate!" he whisper-shouted.

Gio looked around. Had anyone heard him? He couldn't risk saying anything more. He snapped his fingers to get Millie's attention and she ran to his side.

"Chocolate is poison for dogs," Millie told Bean in a soft voice.

"What's poison?" Bean asked. Then he jumped over a plate of cheese and crackers.

Gio was starting to sweat. He made pleading puppy-dog eyes at Millie and she jumped up onto a chair next to Bean.

"Poison makes you throw up!" Millie explained while Gio slowly crept closer to the table. Maybe if she distracted Bean, Gio could just grab him?

Out of the corner of his eye, Gio saw Isa walking toward them.

Please don't take Millie away, please don't take Millie away, he silently begged. How was he going to stop Bean without Millie? And *how* was he going to do any of this in front of Isa?

Isa gave Gio a funny look. He didn't think he'd said anything most dog people wouldn't have said—*yet*.

"What's throw up?" Bean asked. He leaned in close to the cake and sniffed around the edges as if it might be dangerous . . . or incredibly delicious.

Gio glanced between Isa and Millie.

"Throw-up is gross stuff from inside your belly that comes up out of your mouth and makes you want to cry," Millie explained.

"This whole scene makes me want to cry," Houdini chimed in. She hovered around the table to enjoy the chaos.

Bean tilted his head and looked at Millie for a second. "I don't believe you," he said. "This smells good. . . ." He leaned forward, opened his mouth, and—

"Bean!" Gio said firmly. "Leave it!"

Everyone in the living room turned to look at him. Janice held up her phone's camera.

Bean stopped and looked up at Gio, too. "Do you have a treat that tastes better than chocolate cake?" he asked.

"Yes," Gio said. *Yes* was a marker word his mom used whenever a dog did what she'd asked for. Anyone listening would think Gio was just being a good trainer. No one would know he was chatting with the puppy.

Except maybe Isa, who was looking at him now with a big question on her face.

"I got your back, Gio!" Millie jumped off the chair and darted for Isa to distract her. She quickly tugged Isa over to Evie, who was chatting with a young couple by the door.

Bean wagged his tail and ran across the table to Gio.

"Good boy," said Gio. "One, two, three, going down." On three, Gio lifted Bean off the table and set him on the floor.

Bean barked, and drool dripped off his tongue.

"Whatchya got for me?" he asked. His brown tail thumped against the floor.

Gio grabbed a treat from one of the jars on the shelves and placed it on the ground in front of Bean. The puppy gobbled it up in two bites.

"I'm a good boy, I'm a good boy!" Bean jumped around in a circle and sang with his mouth full.

Gio heard clapping and looked around the living room to find a bunch of grown-ups smiling at him. He noticed Gabe come in and head straight for the kitchen—but he couldn't think about that in all the commotion.

I guess they like my skills, Gio thought, blushing.

His mom put her arm around him and turned to the crowd.

"My son is one of the excellent trainers here at Barker's Doghouse," she told their guests.

This would be a good time to show off Bean's skills and help him get adopted, Gio thought.

He squatted down and whispered in Bean's ear. "Do all the tricks you did for me outside—without the skateboard? Humans *love* that kind of stuff."

"Okay!" Bean barked.

Gio stood back up.

"Wanna see what we've been working on?" he asked the crowd. His mom may have been annoying lately, but it felt good to help her out.

The crowd clapped. His mom caught his eye and smiled.

"One, two, three . . ." Gio said.

Bean ran around Gio in a figure eight. Then he

jumped over Gio's arm twice and finished up with a twisting backflip.

Janice caught the whole thing on video, and the people in the living room cheered.

"What a perfect puppy!" one woman exclaimed.

Out of the corner of his eye, Gio saw Millie and Gary rolling around on the ground laughing.

"Everyone thinks you're some kind of dog-training genius..." Millie sputtered.

"... but you just spoke to Bean in plain English!" Gary finished her sentence.

"And *we* taught Bean all those tricks!" Millie was laughing so hard she started to sneeze.

"Well done," said Gio's mom. She looked like she might cry and her arms were outstretched for a hug.

Gio took a giant step backward. Didn't she know she couldn't hug him with so many kids from school around?

"Those were some excellent trainer skills," she said. "You could have a future in this."

Gio rolled his eyes before he could stop himself.

"Yeah, I was good, wasn't I?" Gio said. *But Bean was really good, too.* And then it hit him. He knew *exactly* what they should do if they couldn't find a family to adopt Bean.

"Mom, I know what I want for my birthday!" Gio said. He pulled her into the kitchen and Millie, Bean, and Gary followed. After all, they couldn't resist a good secret.

"Let me guess," his mom said. "You want to leave this open house, go upstairs, and play *Night of the Howling Moon* with your friends?"

Gio smiled.

"Well, always." He took a deep breath in. "But sometimes you have to let go of the thing you've been wanting so you can maybe-hopefully get something even better..."

His mom looked like she might try to hug him again, so Gio kept talking.

"*We* should adopt Bean," Gio blurted out. "I want *us* to be his family."

Out of the corner of his eye, Gio saw Bean do a little dance of joy.

His mom's face fell. Gio felt his heart fall, too.

"Oh. Oh, Gio, I—I was going to tell you—" Her mouth opened and closed like she knew she was in trouble. "The shelter and I have already found Bean a home."

Gio's eyes opened wide. "What? You did? When? With who? Where?"

Before she could answer, the back door banged open. Gabe walked in, tossed an empty plate into the sink, and opened Gio's refrigerator. His cheeks were stuffed with something and he was chewing loudly.

"Epic cookies, Barker," he mumbled between chews. "Got milk?"

CHAPTER FOURTEEN

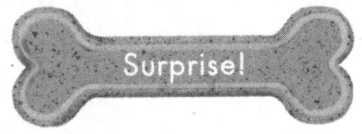

"You ate all the treats!" Gio looked at the crumbs on the plate in the sink. *Who even does that?*

"You ate *all* of them?" Millie repeated. She stared at Gabe. A low growl started in her belly. Her body dipped, her tail went stiff, and she showed her teeth. Millie was ready to pounce.

"Millie, leave it!" said Gio. But Millie didn't listen.

Gio's mom stepped in front of Gabe before Millie could lunge at him. She grabbed Millie's collar and turned her to face away from the boys.

Millie tried to wriggle out of her grip but Julie was too strong.

Instead, Millie snarled and lunged, snapping at the air.

"Well, you certainly have quite an effect on the dogs," Gio's mom told Gabe.

"That was my chance!" Millie howled. "Today was my day! *Isa* was supposed to talk to me—not that stinky bully!"

Isa dashed in from the other room. In one quick movement, she clipped Millie's leash to her harness and led her out into the backyard.

"Quit messing with my dog, Gabe," Isa said on their way out the door.

"What's her problem?" Gabe scoffed. He pulled a carton of milk out of the fridge and looked around for a glass.

Bean nipped at the bottom of Gio's pants.

"What's going on, Gio?" Bean asked. "Why is Millie so mad?" His tail was tucked and his little body was trembling.

That's when Gio fully understood. Gabe might be able to talk to dogs now! *What will he do if he can?*

Gio picked Bean up and turned to his mom. "Mom, we can't let Gabe adopt Bean!"

Gabe was too busy looking through their fridge to disagree.

Gio's mom's eyebrows scrunched in the middle. "Oh Gio, I would hope you'd know me better than—"

The doorbell rang, cutting her off.

"Great, more people," Gio mumbled.

But his mom's face broke into a ginormous smile.

"I think you should get that," said his mom. "It might be your birthday surprise!"

Gio was so confused. *My birthday surprise? I'm still getting a birthday surprise? What is even happening right now?*

His mom turned him around and nudged him toward the front door.

He felt a crowd of humans and dogs following him as he walked.

Janice trained her phone on him. "And here we have a prime example of a caninicus humanus in the wild . . ." she said.

This day could not get any weirder.

As he got closer to the door, he heard the theme

song to *Night of the Howling Moon* playing on someone's phone.

He opened the door and a group of kids shouted, "SURPRISE!"

Gio blinked. Bean barked and wriggled so hard, Gio had to put him down. The puppy ran outside to greet the new guests and jumped up on them for pets. So much for his perfect training.

Gio's friends were standing on the porch holding balloons and presents. Not his new friends from Milton or his doggy friends from the daycare, but his friends from forever—Marco, CharChar, and Jonah.

And they were all there to celebrate Gio.

CHAPTER FIFTEEN

"Happiest best birthday ever!" Char squealed as she handed Gio a box. "We got you cannolis from D'Amatos." She bent down to fuss over Bean.

"And pizza from Carmelo's!" said Marco. He was holding five large pizza boxes.

"And I brought that baseball jersey you left at my house last summer," Jonah said.

Char rolled her eyes. "Jonah's been wearing it."

Jonah shrugged. "It's comfy."

Gio's mom came out. "Surprised?" she asked Gio.

There were no words. Yes, Gio was surprised. Everything he'd wanted for his birthday and thought he wasn't getting was right here on his porch in Milton.

"Got you!" His mom smiled and waggled her eyebrows. "And there's more," she said mysteriously as she took the pizzas and went inside to warm them up in the kitchen.

"Now you're just gloating," Gio said. His birthday wish had come true. What else did he even want?

He reached out to poke Marco's shoulder just to make sure it was all real.

"I can't believe you guys are really here!"

Marco laughed and wrapped an arm about Gio's shoulders.

"Yeah, we all drove down together," he said. "Well, my mom drove us. She's still parking the car."

"It was so much fun!" said Charlotte. She sat down on the ground so Bean could lick her face. "We stopped to see the world's biggest dust bunny."

"It was gross, but cool," said Jonah. He handed Gio a plastic bag with his jersey inside.

Gio was amazed. "I can't believe you guys kept all this a secret."

"We didn't," said Jonah. "Our parents just told us this morning."

"Yeah, there's no way we could have kept a secret this big from our best friend," said Marco. He leaned against the porch railing.

Gio thought about all the secrets he'd been keeping from his best friends.

Then Jonah nudged Charlotte. "Tell him the rest of the surprise," he insisted.

Char glanced at Marco, who nodded.

"Okay!" She jumped up and pulled Gio over to the porch swing.

"Well, we came for your birthday . . ." Char said, grinning.

". . . but also to pick up my new dog," Marco completed the sentence. He smiled the biggest smile Gio had seen since the time they found an old arrowhead buried in their schoolyard.

Did he even hear that right? "What?" said Gio.

There was a thump on the window and Gio looked back to see Gary and Houdini pawing at the glass, panting. Millie squeezed in between them. All their little tails were wagging.

Had they known all along?

"My little brothers are finally old enough to have a dog," Marco said. "My mom called you an inspiración. She said we can adopt Bean as long as you teach me how to take care of him. We can do online training sessions together!"

"*You're* gonna be Bean's new family?" Gio couldn't believe it. Bean was going to live with his best friend. His best *human* friend.

"Your mom is *reeeaaally* good at surprises," Jonah said. He wrapped an arm around Gio's shoulders.

"If you can part with him." Marco smiled. "You seem pretty attached to the little guy."

Gio looked down at Bean, who was hiding under the wicker coffee table.

"Don't be scared, Bean, it's okay," Gio said. "It's more than okay. It's the best plan ever!" He crouched down next to the puppy and gently scratched under his chin.

Gio was going to miss seeing him every day, but it was such a relief to know that Bean was going to the best home Gio could think of.

Wait until Isa finds out! he thought.

Marco knelt down beside them, too.

Bean slowly crawled out from under the table and sniffed Marco's knees.

"You were on the computer! You smell like burgers." Bean's tail wagged and smacked Gio in the face.

Marco reached out a hand to pet Bean.

"Ouch!" he exclaimed.

"Oops," said Bean. "I was excited."

Gio laughed. "Oh, yeah, you gotta be careful," he said. "This guy's a little land shark."

CHAPTER SIXTEEN

"It's just like you told me, Gio," Bean said. "Sometimes when you leave it, you get something even better!"

Bean was snuggled up between Gio and Marco in the mini treehouse in Gio's backyard.

Gio smiled. This was turning out to be a better birthday than he'd ever imagined.

All his friends—from home, and school, and soccer—were hanging out together. Isa, Jonah, and Gary had joined in the soccer game while CharChar showed Evie how to catch gummy fish in her mouth.

Janice had helped Gio's mom move the pizza, chips, and soda onto the back deck. Then they went back inside to wrap up the open house.

They'd already signed up three new dogs for Barker's Doghouse, including a French bulldog.

Lots of things were changing. But some of the best things were staying the same.

Millie came running over to Gio with a ball in her mouth.

She dropped it at the base of the treehouse.

"Let's pretend to play fetch so we can talk!" she said.

"Be right back," Gio told Marco and Bean.

He followed Millie to the far end of the yard. Then he leaned down to pick up the ball. "I'm sorry the treats didn't work out, Millie. We'll try again," he whispered.

"Let's bake some more tomorrow!" she said, and nuzzled Gio's cheek.

Gio had to smile. Millie might be able to let some things go, but she never gave up.

Millie looked out at all the dogs and humans playing together in the yard. Avocado slide-tackled Jonah and they both got covered in dirt. "Isn't this the best surprise ever?" she asked.

Gio tilted his head. Something wasn't quite right.

Millie didn't seem surprised at all. Had she known all along? He gave her some side-eye.

But she just looked up at him with her tongue sticking out of the side of her mouth.

Gio shook his head. He *had* been really surprised. And it felt kind of great.

And Millie was right. If he'd insisted on going

home he'd have missed out on having all his friends—old and new—hanging out together right here.

His face broke into a big, wide grin. He'd just remembered something.

Gio held up a finger as if to say wait. Then he ran inside and came back with a small box. It was all wrapped up like a present.

He tossed it toward Millie.

"Go get it!" he said.

"A present for *me*? On *your* birthday?" Millie ran over to the box and tore it open with her teeth and paws.

Inside, was a yellow, rubbery, squeaky banana.

"Squeaky banana!" She took her new toy between her teeth and squeaked out the melody to the happy birthday song.

Then she put it down so she could lick the side of Gio's face.

"Hey Bean," she called. "Wanna play?"

"Woof woof! Sure do!" Bean leaped off the treehouse to join her.

A few minutes later, Gio's mom came out of the house carrying out the chocolate cake she'd made, only now it had candles on it. Everyone crammed onto the back deck to sing.

"Happy birthday to you . . ." Isa and Char got everyone singing along.

Gabe stood awkwardly by the back door.

Gio was still too mad at him to invite him to join in.

"Yo, Gio, this dog is really good at soccer." Mason said after Gio had blown out the candles. He rubbed the top of Avocado's head. "He should be the team's mascot!"

"Or assistant coach," Harrison said. "He's tough. I've never dribbled so fast in my life!"

Avocado howled in agreement.

Gabe covered his ears. "Yo, doesn't this dog ever take a break? If I had a dog, it would know when to settle down."

"Don't be a goober, Gabe," Mason said. "You know you would love on a puppy."

"Hehe, Gabe the Goober," Char joked. Then she leaned over to Gio. "You need us to take care of this guy?" she asked.

"You know we've always got your back, right?" Jonah said. "No matter what."

"I'm good," Gio told his friends. "Gabe's all bark and no bite."

Just then, a scraggly gray dog with an underbite walked slowly out the back door and stopped to stretch.

"Felix!" Millie called out. She jumped off Isa's lap and ran over to the terrier. "Where have you been?"

"In my fort," said Felix.

"Have you been hiding in the corner of the living room since the puppy arrived?" Gary asked.

"Till you all started making a ruckus!" he growled.

Gio watched Gabe's face. *Does he hear them talking? Does he understand?*

"Yo, where did this mutt come from? He looks like Oscar the Grouch got stuck in the lawnmower." Gabe laughed.

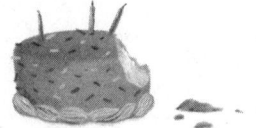

Felix quietly lifted his leg over Gabe's sneakers.

"Gross!" Gabe exclaimed as the warm liquid seeped into his canvas sneakers. "Now I gotta go home and change. Mason, you coming?"

"Nah," said Mason. "I'm going to hang out a while. But I'll catch up with you tomorrow."

When Gabe stomped off, no one even said good-bye.

Gio sat down on the steps next to Marco and called Bean over.

"I'm gonna miss you, Beanie," Gio said as he rubbed behind Bean's ears. "But you're getting the best family. They have a yard and three kids and a really awesome mom who will let you sit on the couch and eat steak once in a while."

"It's true," Marco told Bean. "My mom is going to spoil you!"

Bean rolled over onto his back so Marco could rub his tummy.

"Will you come visit us, Gio?" Bean asked.

"Yes, and we'll video chat all the time," Gio said.

Marco looked between Gio and the pup. "You think he understands?" he asked.

Gio nodded. "One hundred percent. Just wait until you hear the secret I've been keeping."

Maria Bea Alfano is a writer and artist who lives in New York City. She's taught art and soccer to preschoolers, reading to first graders, writing to adults, and ESL to middle schoolers in Spain. But her favorite job is raising her doggy BFF who loves agility, hiking, and making new friends. This is Maria's first fiction series.

Want to know how it all started?
Check out *Fetch!* And look for
High Five!, coming soon.